Caillou®

Every Drop Counts!

Adaptation of the animated series: Sarah Margaret Johanson
Illustrations: CINAR Animation; adapted by Eric Sévigny

Caillou was always learning interesting new things at day care. Today he was learning about water.

"Water falls from the sky as rain. It waters plants and eventually runs back into lakes and rivers," said Miss Martin. "Then it evaporates — that means it turns into a gas, like air — and rises up, where it collects in clouds and gets ready to...?"

"Fall down like rain again!"
Clementine called out.

"Right," Miss Martin said.

"Wow!" Caillou exclaimed.

"What do we use water for?" Miss Martin asked.

"Drinking," Leo said.

"Taking a bath," Clementine said.

"Brushing our teeth and washing dishes," Caillou said.

"Yes. We use a lot of water every day, but it's important not to waste any, so that there will be enough for all those who need it – people, and animals, and even plants," Miss Martin explained.

"Miss Martin, how can I use less water?" Caillou asked.

"We'll talk about that on Monday, but why don't you see what ideas you can think of?"

When he got home, Caillou went into the kitchen.

"Hi, Daddy. What are you doing?"

"I'm just washing the lettuce for dinner," Daddy replied.

"No, Daddy! Don't!" Caillou said. "Miss Martin says we should use less water."

Daddy smiled. "Well, she is right about that, but I've got to wash the lettuce so we can eat it."

At bath time, Caillou said, "I'm going to save water by not taking any more baths."

Mommy looked at him kindly, but sternly. "I know you're trying to do a good thing, Caillou, but you still have to take your bath." She turned the tap on. "You're going to have to think of another way to save water."

"Okay," Caillou frowned.

This was harder than he thought it would be.

Caillou walked over to the sink.
"I could stop brushing my teeth."
"No, but we could save water by
not filling the tub so full and by
turning off the tap while we brush
our teeth."
Caillou looked at the tap on the sink.
"Mommy, the tap is dripping."
"You know, we can save water by
fixing that leaky tap."
Caillou looked doubtful. "It's just
dripping a teeny-tiny bit."

"It's not such a teeny-tiny bit when you add up all those drops. I've got an idea." Mommy pulled out a small bucket and placed it in the sink. "Why don't we collect the drips overnight and see how much water a dripping tap wastes? It'll be an experiment."

"Yeah, okay!" Caillou said. He was excited at the idea of finally finding a way to save water.

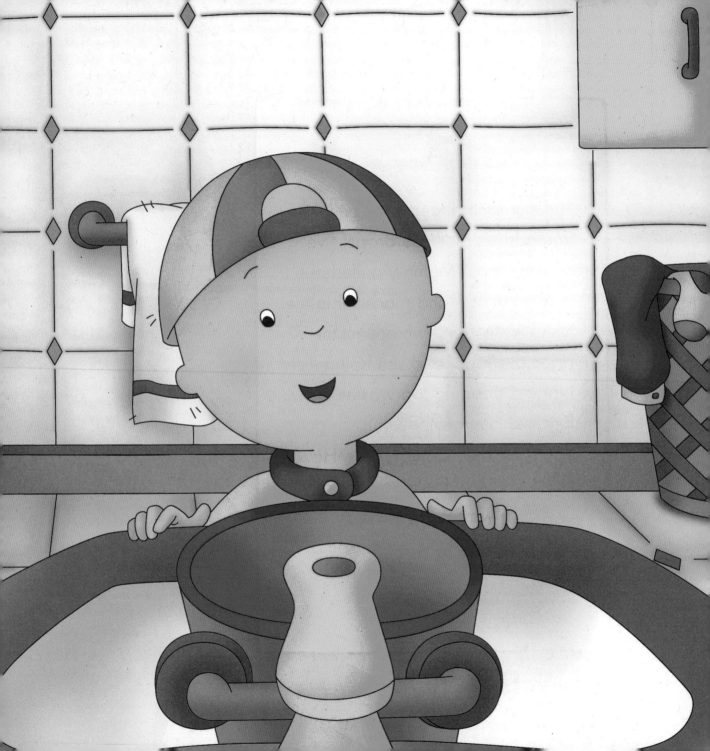

The next morning Caillou rushed to see how much water was in the bucket.

"Mommy, the bucket is full!"

"And that's not all. I emptied it twice during the night into this bigger bucket," Mommy said. "All that water would have just dripped down the drain and been wasted."

"Wow, that's a lot of water!" Caillou exclaimed. "Maybe other taps are leaking, too. I'm going to go check."

That afternoon Caillou was looking out the window. The clouds were dripping water just like the leaky tap. Caillou had an idea and ran to the kitchen. He went straight to the lower cupboards and collected an armful of pots and pans.

"What are you up to, Caillou?" Daddy asked.

"I'm going to save a lot of water!" Mommy and Daddy watched through the window as Caillou carefully placed the pots and pans around the yard.

"What a smart idea, Caillou!"
Mommy said.
"I collected lots and lots of water."
He handed Mommy a pot of
water.
"I'll use this to water my plants,"
Mommy said. "And to wash the
floor or the windows."
"Or fill Gilbert's water dish,"
Caillou said.
"Instead of using pots and pans,
we could get a really big barrel to
collect rain in," Daddy suggested.

On Monday, Caillou told the class about the ideas he had had over the weekend to help save water. He showed them a picture.

"So Daddy bought a rain barrel like this, and we put it in the backyard, and the next time it rains the barrel will fill up with rainwater," he explained.

"That's wonderful, Caillou!" Miss Martin said.

Caillou was very proud of his ideas for saving water. Every little drop adds up!

Text adapted by Sarah Margaret Johanson from the scenario of the CAILLOU animated
film series produced by Cookie Jar Entertainment Inc. (© 1997 Caillou Productions (2004) Inc.,
a subsidiary of Cookie Jar Entertainment Inc.).
All rights reserved.
Original scenario written by Kim Thompson.
Original episode no 514: Caillou saves water.
Illustrations taken from the television series CAILLOU and adapted by Eric Sévigny.
Art Direction: Monique Dupras

The PBS KIDS logo is a registered mark of PBS and is used with permission.

We acknowledge the financial support of the Government of Canada through
the Canada Book Fund for our publishing activities.

Canadian Patrimoine
Heritage canadien

We acknowledge the support of the Ministry of Culture and Communications
of Quebec and SODEC for the publication and promotion of this book.

SODEC
Québec

Bibliothèque et Archives nationales du Québec and Library
and Archives Canada cataloguing in publication

Johanson, Sarah Margaret, 1968-
Caillou: every drop counts!
(Ecology club)
For children aged 3 and up.

ISBN 978-2-89450-772-8

1. Water efficiency - Juvenile literature. I. Sévigny, Eric. II. Title. III. Title: Every drop counts!.

TD388.J63 2011   j333.91'17   C2010-942000-4

Legal deposit: 2011

The use of entirely recycled paper
produced locally, containing
chlorine-free 100% post-consumer
content, saved 69 mature trees.

FSC® Recycled
Supporting responsible use
of forest resources
www.fsc.org Cert no. SGS-COC-004340
© 1996 Forest Stewardship Council

Printed in Canada
10 9 8 7 6 5 4 3 2 1